Anywhere
Farm

For Ellen and Van
P. R.

For Sebastian
G. B. K.

First edition 2017

Library of Congress Catalog Card Number pending
ISBN 978-0-7636-7499-1

16 17 18 19 20 21 CCP 10 9 8 7 6 5 4 3 2 1

Printed in Shenzhen, Guangdong, China

This book was typeset in Clichee and Berlinner Grotesk.
The illustrations were done in mixed media.

Candlewick Press
99 Dover Street
Somerville, Massachusetts 02144

visit us at www.candlewick.com

Anywhere Farm

Phyllis Root

illustrated by G. Brian Karas

CANDLEWICK PRESS

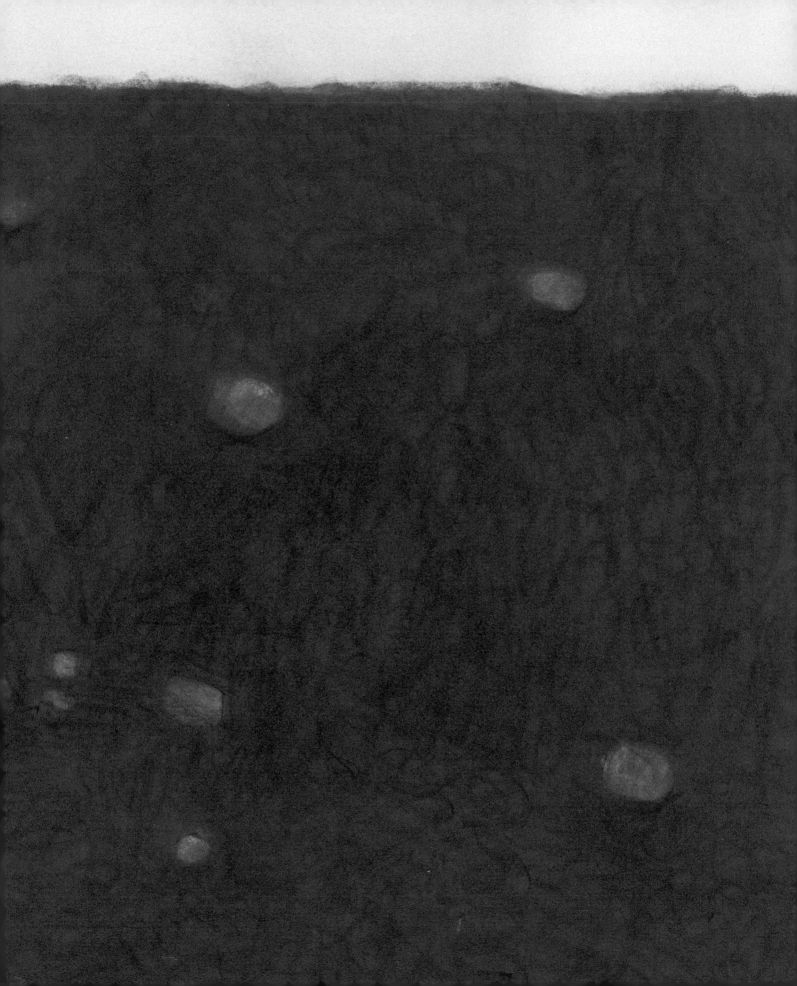

For an anywhere farm,
here's all that you need:

soil

and sunshine,

some water,

a seed.

Fat seed or skinny seed,
pointy or round,
tenderly tuck it
down into the ground.

Then you watch and you wait.
You water. You weed.
Your seed will sprout out
at its own seedy speed.

And you'll have an anywhere,
anywhere farm.

Where can
you plant
your
anywhere
farm?

NO DUMPING

An old empty lot
makes a good growing plot.
But a pan or a bucket,
a pot or a shoe,
a bin or a tin
or a window will do.

Plant a farm in a crate!
Plant a farm in a cup!
In a box on a balcony
ten stories up!

Plant a farm in a truck!

In a box on a bike!

Plant an anywhere farm
anywhere that you like.

Anywhere that you have
some soil, some seed,
some sunshine and water.
(That's all that you need.)

For your

anywhere,

anywhere,

anywhere
farm.

What can
you plant
on your
anywhere
farm?

Kale in a pail.

Corn in a horn.

Beets and zucchini,   jicama, broccoli,
oregano, beans,   radishes, greens.

Tomatoes, potatoes, peppers, and peas.

On your anywhere farm, plant whatever you please.

You might see a monarch,
a ladybug,
bees,
hummingbirds, cardinals,
fat chickadees.

Your neighbors might come.
When they see what you've grown,
they might want an anywhere farm
of their own.

You might give them some seeds
that they plant in a can,
a carton, a washtub, an old frying pan.

In a boat or a boot
or right in their yard.
Anybody can do it.
You've showed it's not hard.

With your farm in a basket,
and mine on a chair,

with soil and sunshine and water and care,
one day all our anywhere farms anywhere
might turn into . . .

an everywhere farm —

everywhere.

Where does it all start?
What do you need?

Just one farmer — you —
and one little seed.